mario makes a move

Jill McElmurry

schwartz & wade books · new york

To my amazing family

Mario liked to invent amazing moves.

Twirly Ballet Arms

Tail, Don't Fail

Bowling Ball

Crazy Wave

Upside-Down Around

Rocket to Mars

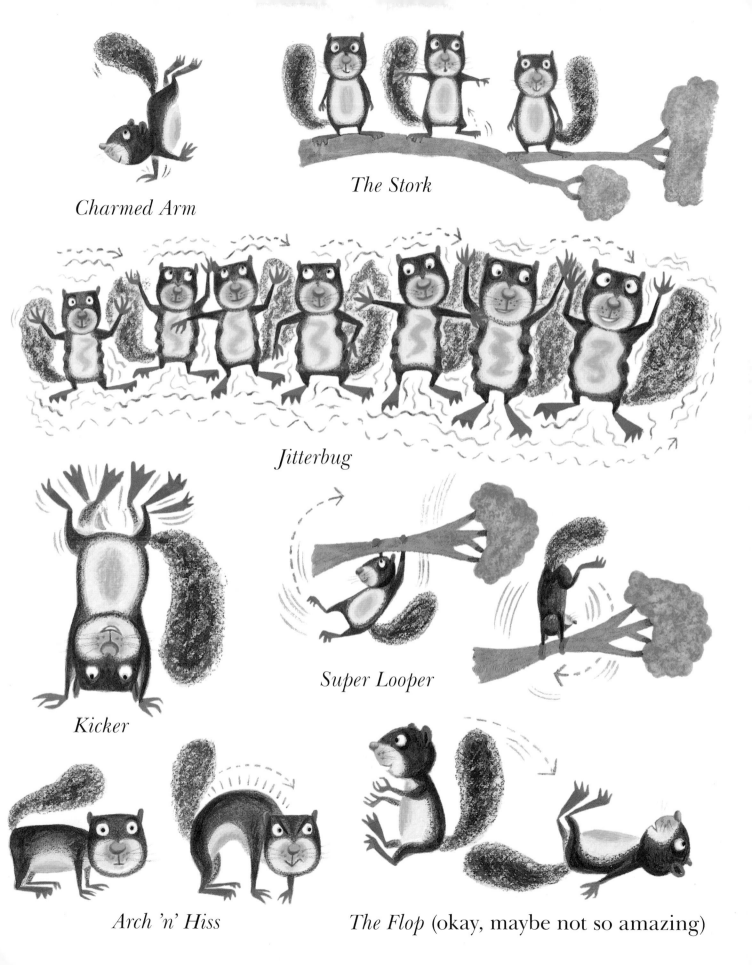

Charmed Arm

The Stork

Jitterbug

Kicker

Super Looper

Arch 'n' Hiss

The Flop (okay, maybe not so amazing)

"Look! Look!" said Mario.

"Amazing!" said Mario's dad.

"Artistic!" said Mario's mom.

"Astonishing!" said his grandpa.

"Alarming!" said his auntie.

"Aaaaa!" said his cousins, who didn't know words.

HOW To
Do MARIO's
AMAZING
MOVE

1.

"Look! Look!" Mario said to Isabelle.

"That's nice," said Isabelle.

"NICE?" said Mario. "I think you mean amazing. Or astonishing, maybe."

"Hmmm," said Isabelle.

"It's called the Amazing Amazer," said Mario.

"Oh," said Isabelle.

"Aren't you amazed?" said Mario.

"I guess," said Isabelle.

"You don't know an amazing move when you see one," said Mario. "I'd like to see *you* try it."

"No problem," said Isabelle.

How to Do Isabelle's Amazing Move

A.

B.

C.

D.

E.

F.

G.

H.

I.

J.

K.

L.

"I don't think we can be friends anymore," said Mario.

"Why not?" said Isabelle, straightening her glasses.

"Because you stole my move," he said.

"I did not steal your move," she said.

"Did so!" said Mario.

"That wasn't your move," said Isabelle. "That was *my* move."

"You can't have a move!" said Mario.

"Why not?" said Isabelle. "Anyone can have a move.

"See?"

"Oh, dear," said Mario.

"What are you doing?" said Isabelle the next day.

"Finding sticks," said Mario.

"Why?"

"It's my new hobby," said Mario.

"What about your amazing move?"

"Anyone can have an amazing move," said Mario. "*I* have amazing sticks."

"Hmmm," said Isabelle.

"Aren't you amazed?" said Mario.

"They're just sticks."

"You don't know an amazing stick when you see one," said Mario.

"Your move is more amazing than that stick," said Isabelle.

"My move was dumb. I got rid of it," said Mario.

"Too bad. I wanted you to teach it to me."

"Really?" said Mario.

"Really," said Isabelle.

"But you said it was NICE," said Mario.

"I meant to say it was elegant."

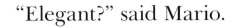

"Elegant?" said Mario.

"And graceful."
"Graceful?!" said Mario.
He dropped his stick.

"You know," said Mario,
"I want you to teach me
your move, too!"

So Isabelle taught Mario her move . . .
and Mario taught Isabelle the
Amazing Amazer . . .

And then they mashed the two moves together and invented the Even More Amazingly Amazing Amazer.

And everyone was amazed.

IF YOU ARE A SQUIRREL

1. Your brain is the size of a walnut. ←walnut

2. You Probably Live in a tree.

3. You like to eat acorns, nuts, seeds, and roots, and sometimes you'll even eat insects, caterpillars, or BABY BIRDS!

4. You have a bushy tail.

5. You have FOUR FRONT teeth that never STOP Growing.

6. You have THUMBS on your feet.
Thumb   BRANCH

7. Also, you sweat through your feet.

8. You are one of hundreds of species in a number of families, including Tree squirrels, ground squirrels, and FLYING squirrels.

9. Your first ancestor Lived about 35 million Years AGO!

10. You can run as fast as 20 miles per HOUR.

11. You bury your Food, although sometimes You forGet wHere.

12. You ARE considered cute by some and pesky by otHERS.

13. YOU MAKE amazing moves.
↑   ↑   ↑ ↑   ↑   ↑

Copyright © 2012 by Jill McElmurry

All rights reserved. Published in the United States by Schwartz & Wade Books, an imprint of Random House Children's Books, a division of Random House, Inc., New York.

Schwartz & Wade Books and the colophon are trademarks of Random House, Inc.

Visit us on the Web! randomhouse.com/kids

Educators and librarians, for a variety of teaching tools, visit us at randomhouse.com/teachers

Library of Congress Cataloging-in-Publication Data
McElmurry, Jill.
Mario makes a move / Jill McElmurry.—1st ed.
p. cm.
Summary: Mario and Isabelle, two squirrels, teach each other their amazing dance moves. Includes facts about squirrels.
ISBN 978-0-375-86854-2 (trade) — ISBN 978-0-375-96854-9 (glb)
[1. Squirrels—Fiction. 2. Dance—Fiction.] I. Title.
PZ7.M4784485Mar 2012
[E]—dc23
2011011014

The text of this book is set in Baskerville.
The illustrations were rendered in gouache on watercolor paper.
Book design by Becky Terhune and Rachael Cole
MANUFACTURED IN MALAYSIA
10 9 8 7 6 5 4 3 2 1
First Edition

Random House Children's Books supports the First Amendment and celebrates the right to read.